Come Be with Me

Other books by

Blue Mountain Press INC

Come Into the Mountains, Dear Friend
by Susan Polis Schutz

I Want to Laugh, I Want to Cry
by Susan Polis Schutz

Peace Flows from the Sky
by Susan Polis Schutz

Someone Else to Love
by Susan Polis Schutz

I'm Not That Kind of Girl
by Susan Polis Schutz

Yours If You Ask
by Susan Polis Schutz

The Best Is Yet to Be

Step to the Music You Hear, Vol. I

The Language of Friendship

The Language of Love

The Language of Happiness

The Desiderata of Happiness
by Max Ehrmann

Whatever Is, Is Best
by Ella Wheeler Wilcox

Poor Richard's Quotations
by Benjamin Franklin

I Care About Your Happiness
by Kahlil Gibran/Mary Haskell

My Life and Love Are One
by Vincent Van Gogh

I Wish You Good Spaces
by Gordon Lightfoot

We Are All Children Searching for Love
by Leonard Nimoy

Catch Me with Your Smile
by Peter McWilliams

Creeds to Love and Live By

On the Wings of Friendship

Think of Me Kindly
by Ludwig van Beethoven

You've Got a Friend
Carole King

Come Be
with Me

A collection of poems by
Leonard Nimoy

Designed by SandPiper Studios, Inc.

Blue Mountain Press ™

Boulder, Colorado

Library of Congress Number: 78-59098
ISBN: 0-88396-033-8

First Printing: September, 1978

Designed by SandPiper Studios, Inc.

Blue Mountain Press INC.

P.O. Box 4549, Boulder, Colorado 80306

CONTENTS

Introduction

I have a garden which I love. Once in awhile it looks perfect. All the watering, feeding, pruning and love add up to a moment of beauty.

Then I think . . . if only I could keep it this way, preserve this moment forever. But my garden is alive. Time and seasons bring changes. Living things must change.

A life is like a garden. Perfect moments can be had, but not preserved, except in memory.

This book is dedicated to a thought, not new, but durable . . . I am a living thing which must change. If I can accept the changes, I can accept myself, and when I accept myself I can enjoy the changes and the beauty of the changes in the garden of my life.

There is no peace
    Without harmony
No harmony
    Without music

There is no music
    Without song
No song
    Without beauty

There is no beauty
    Without laughter
No laughter
    Without joy

There is no joy
    Without kindness
No kindness
    Without caring

No caring
    Without love
No love
    Without you

I love you
Not for what
I want you to be
But for what you are

I loved you then
For what you were
I love you now
For what you have become

I miss you
And not only you

I miss what I am
When you are here . . .

Come
        Be with me

        Let your mind
                Float free
        Across the space
                Of our separation

Let it join
        With mine
For an eternal
        Moment

        Who are better
                Joined?
        Those who are together
        Each thinking
                Of other people
                In other places

Or we
        Who are in other places
                Thinking of each other

I may not be the fastest
I may not be the tallest
            Or the strongest

I may not be the best
Or the brightest

    But one thing I can do better
    Than anyone else . . .

    That is

    To be me

Like a snapshot
　　You develop
Unlike a snapshot . . .
　　You never stop

When you touch me
　I am deeply touched
Far deeper than the
　Depth of skin or flesh

You touch the core
　The secret cave
　　Of my being

You touch the dream place
　That some call heart
　Some call soul

For me
　　It has no name
　　　　But me
When you touch me
　　You touch
　　　　Me

Come
My darling
Love me
Touch me deep
As only you can do

I have waited
Wanted
Hungered
Needed
God, I have needed
Your presence
Your nearness

I admit

Not with shame
But with pride

I need your presence
I need your touch
I need . . .
You.

May you be guided by
    The heavenly light

May your dreams
    Become solid and sound

May your goals be
    Well chosen and surely found

May your deeds be touched
    By decency and grace

And above all,
    May you find the time
        To be kind

I have walked alone
   Seeking answers

I have lived alone
   Chasing dreams

I have tried
   To prove my worth
To worthless judges

I have cried my pain
   In silent screams

            I have been
               Sometimes served
               A touch of kindness

            I have wandered
               In golden fields
                  Of grace

            I have been
               Released by honest
                  Laughter

            I have touched
               The Western Wall
               Of the Holy Place

I have soared
Alone
Above the cloud heads

I have walked
The deep dark
Tunnels of the earth

I have dined
With mystics
And with prophets

I have heard
The pain of woman
Giving birth

I have been
Sought after
As a teacher

I have been
Refused
The Laurel Wreath

I have heard
The thunder blast
Of sunrise

I have watched
The final touch
Of death

I have played
The rules
Set by the master

Though often I didn't
Understand the game

I have worn
More masks than
I remember

I have been
A face without
A name

And when
Like you
  I ask
    The final question

      Who on earth
        Am I supposed
          To be?

I always
Come full circle
  To the answer

      Me

    Only me

  Always me . . .

Trying to write a poem . . .

This poem
   May not rhyme . . .
Then again it may

I can't be sure
   'Cause I don't know
What it is I want to say

My head and heart
   Are full of thoughts
   Wanting to be words

I'm trying to find
   A way to say these things
   That should be heard (s)

Sometimes a poem
   Springs to life
   Sometimes it's hard to do

Yesterday the words came fast
Today they seem to stumble (through)

Still I feel
It's worth a try
Because I like
  To write 'em

So I'll go on
With words of love
Instead of trying
  To fight 'em . . .

    Hooray!!

I am me

You are you

Our love

Is us

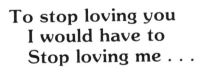

To stop loving you
I would have to
Stop loving me . . .

In the desert
    I learned about heat

In the snow
    I learned about cold

When you left
    I learned about lonely

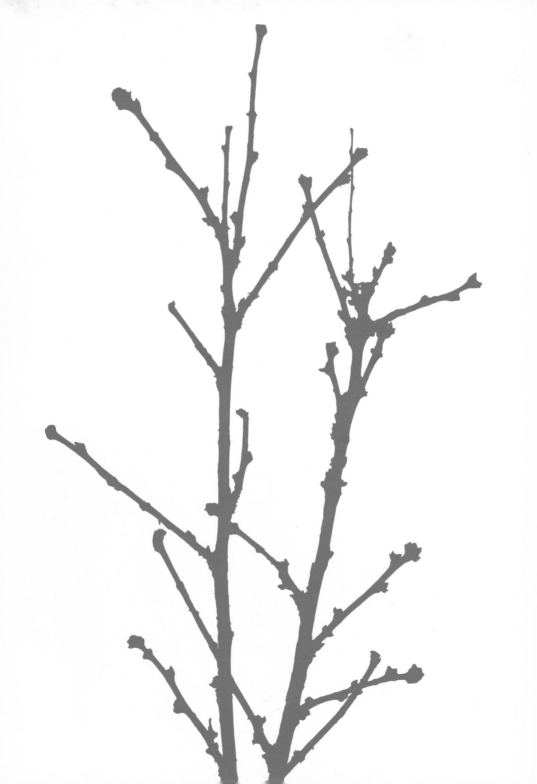

The truth is
  We cannot give love

Love is
  A condition
It can have a beginning
  And an end

It can have a life cycle
  Like a flower

But unlike a flower
  We cannot pluck it
From one person and
  Hand it to another

        Because we love
        We trust
          And with trust
              We love

        I love you

            I do not give you love
        As a reward
            To be given only
                When things are right

              Our love
              Simply is there
              Over
                    Around
                        Embracing us both
                          Always

If love can be withdrawn
It never was

My love for you is not a gift
   To you
            It is a gift
                  To me

Without others
    I am
        Alone

Without you
    I am
        Lonesome

My love is a garden

You are the sun

When you shine
On my garden
   It grows

You feed it
With your smile

You warm it
With your heart

You bless it
With your being

When friends say,
   My, you have a
      beautiful garden

   I look at you,
      and smile.

Blessed
        Are they
Who have learned
        To let themselves
                Be loved

Rocket ships
    Are exciting
But so are roses
    On a birthday

Computers are exciting
    But so is a sunset

And logic
    Will never replace
                    Love

    Sometimes I wonder
    Where I belong
        In the future
                Or
        In the past

    I guess I'm just
        An old-fashioned
                Space-man

I'll be home

    I'll bring you
    Kiss caresses
      Aged with longing

    Eye to eye
    Hand in hand

I'll be with you

    At home
      To share the evening quiet
      And the bird song of the morning

I'll be at home

    With you
      To share
        Our love

If there is
Nothing more than this
   It is enough

We have flown
      The heights

We have rested
   On the crest

We have seen
      The sights of wonder
      The glorious days
      The peaceful nights

We have touched and traveled
Deep into time
      And far beyond the stars

For we have loved
      And who
         Can ask for more?

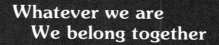

Whatever we are
   We belong together

Wherever we are
   We will find each other

Whoever we are
   We are
      Forever one

If all the deeds of man
        Were grains of sand
And if all those grains
        Of sand were deposited
On a balance scale

    If one side of the scale
        Were the deeds
            Which ennoble humanity
And the other side weighed
        The deeds which degrade
        The individual

        Would you not
            Count it as a blessing
            To be given the choice
            Each day
                To drop a few grains
                On the side of decency?

So this is the
   Blessed opportunity
   Provided to each of us
         Each day
     To tip the scale
     With a few small grains
     Of kindness
       With a smile
         With a word of encouragement
        A promise kept
          Or an offer of help
          At a moment of need

Let me not take for granted

An act of kindness

An offering of love

The glory of human courage

A sign of respect

A phrase of beautiful music

A decent soul

The beauty of a blossom

And above all,

You.

You are the dream
    I dream

You are the sun
    I seek

You are
    My shade

You are the rest
    I sleep

    You are the peace
    I yearn for

You are
    My hope,
    My love

Sweet is
  The sunbreak
  After the rain

Welcome is
  The breeze
  That follows the heat

Warm is
  The fire
  Against the snow

Yet none
  So precious
  As your smile
That says

  Welcome home . . .

  After we've
  Been apart

About the Author

If a man is measured by the various dimensions of his character, and by the integrity and love that are expressed in the fulfillment of each facet, Leonard Nimoy is surely one of the world's "special" people.

Most people recognize Leonard from his character role in television's Star Trek. But the millions of fans who think that they know Leonard Nimoy because they know "Mr. Spock" will discover an added dimension to Leonard's character within the pages of this book. However, the admiration and following that Nimoy has received as a result of his various roles attest to the fact that he is a superb actor.

Broadway, Hollywood, writer and director, singer and actor — the "public" Leonard Nimoy is an artist of the highest regard. In addition to being recognized as an educated and entertaining lecturer, Leonard feels at home in the roles of both teacher and student. After having taught at various acting schools and at Synanon for a time, he has recently completed his Master's Degree in education at Antioch College.

A glance at his credits and activities reveals the "public" side of Leonard — the side that is an extremely busy man, thriving on challenge, variety and professionalism. It has only been in recent years that the "private" Leonard Nimoy has emerged as a well-known poet and photographer.

Ironically perhaps, Leonard's own poems and his richly creative expressions communicate more about the man than any observer could ever hope to say. Thematically, Leonard seems especially aware of our place in space and time, and his poetry often exudes an honest and open intimacy with everyman. On the other hand, Leonard's intense devotion to the special people in his life — people like his wife, Sandi, and their two children — instinctively shines through in shared and private moments. As a reflection of the man, the poetry of Leonard Nimoy is interwoven with passion and compassion, a free-spirited sense of wonder and a deep, human sentiment.